Ceri & Deri – Pudding for Dessert
Published in Great Britain in 2021 by Graffeg Limited.

Graffeg Limited, 24 Stradey Park Business Centre, Mwrwg Road, Llangennech, Llanelli, Carmarthenshire, SA14 8YP, Wales, UK.
Tel: 01554 824000. www.graffeg.com.

A CIP Catalogue record for this book is available from the British Library.

ISBN 9781914079269

1 2 3 4 5 6 7 8 9

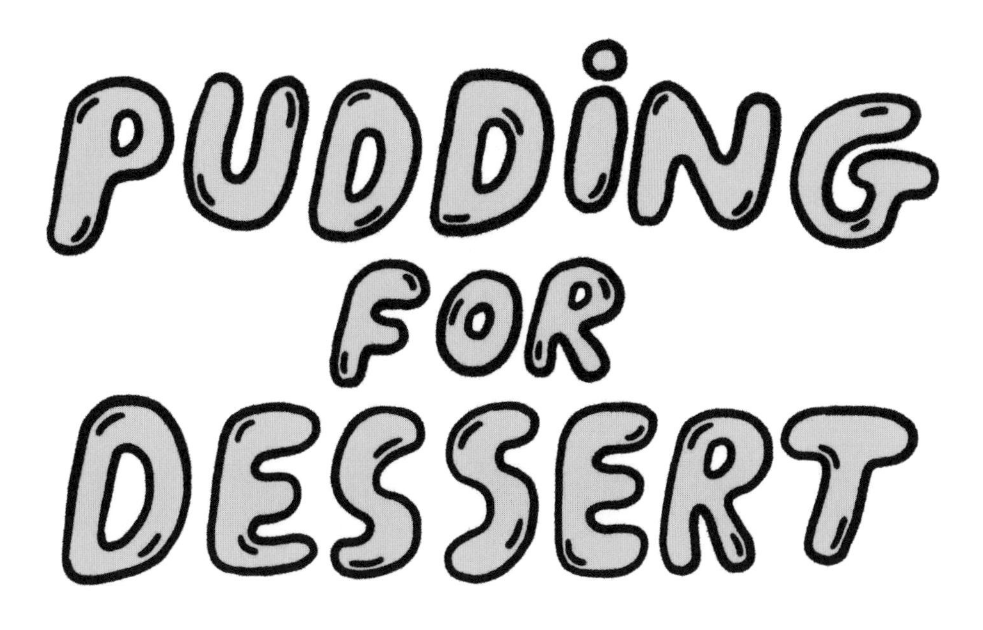

MAX LOW

GRAFFEG

Ceri is a cat. Deri is a Dog.

Ceri has stripes and Deri has spots.

They live in a small town near a small mountain and they do everything together.

They are best friends.

Ceri and Deri love sweet food. There are two shops in town they enjoy visiting more than anywhere else; Delwen's Domain of Desserts and Peredur's Pudding Palace.

They go to both. They go for banana splits, carrot cake and ice cream floats at Delwen's, and for banana splits, carrot cake and ice cream floats at Peredur's.

ne to
TOWN!
opulation: YUM!

DELWEN'S
OF DESSERTS
OPEN
Pere

The two shops sit next to each other on the street like two kingdoms of konfectionary.

But today this peaceful scene is broken by much hoo-ha.

Delwen and Peredur are having an argument.

'A TRIFLE IS A DESSERT! FACT!'

'NO, A TRIFLE IS A PUDDING, AND YOU KNOW IT!'

'NEVER! I WOULD RATHER EAT LENTILS THAN A PUDDING!'

'YOU TAKE THAT BACK! I REFUSE TO BELIEVE IN DESSERT. PUDDING FOREVER!'

OPE

‘Excuse me,’ Ceri asks Delwen politely, ‘can we have two banana splits please?’

‘OH, DESSERT SYMPATHISERS IS IT? WHO KNEW THAT EVERY TIME YOU’RE IN MY SHOP YOU’RE DREAMING OF DESSERTS?!’ shouts Peredur.

‘No, we just go to Delwen’s first because it’s first on the street. You have bigger seats which we can lie down on when we’re full...’

‘OH, MY SEATS AREN’T BIG ENOUGH IS IT? WHO KNEW THAT EVERYTIME YOU’RE IN MY SHOP YOU’RE ACTUALLY DREAMING OF PEREDUR’S BIG SEATS?!’ shouts Delwen.

Ceri and Deri feel bad, even though they haven’t done anything wrong. Even worse, they are hungry.

Delwen and Peredur start hurling their delicious treats at each other.

'YOU DIRTY DESSERT DICTATOR!' shouts Peredur, chucking an ice cream sundae.

'YOU PERNICIOUS PUDDING PERSON!' shouts Delwen, chucking an apple pie.

‘Now then, now then. What’s all this then?’ It’s Detective Inspector Nigel.

‘Ah, here’s the policeman! He’ll put a stop to this craziness,’ says Deri.

‘DESSERTS! HAH! I’M A PUDDING BOY! PUD! PUD! PUD!’ shouts D.I. Nigel, smooshing a bakewell tart into Delwen’s face.

PEN

'I am here to resolve this disturbance.' It's the mayor, surely she will calm everyone down?

Nope.

'ALL HAIL THE DESSERT! POO TO PUDDINGS!' she roars, hurling a strawberry cheesecake at Peredur.

Psteve the Psychiatrist arrives to help...

'DESSERT MUNCHING LOSERS! IT'S PUDDING TIME!' he wails.

General Jenny comes to the rescue...

'PUDDINGS ARE GROSS! I AM A DESSERTER FOR LIFE!' she booms.

Mel the Member of Parliament rushes to the scene...

'PUDDINGS FOR PRIME-MINISTER!' she hollers.

ne to
1 TOW
opulati

Soon everyone in the town has taken a side and is chucking tasty treats at each other.

It's a full-on food fight!

Ceri and Deri hate to see food go to waste and launch themselves into the air, attempting to block the flying feast with their mouths.

Ceri catches an apple pie from Peredur and an ice cream sundae from Delwen, while Deri munches on Delwen's lemon drizzle cake and Peredur's black forest gateau.

'Woah,' says Ceri. 'This is the best thing I've ever eaten!'

'WOAH,' says Deri. 'This is even better than that!'

Soon everyone stops throwing food at each other and starts eating it, because the combination of Delwen's desserts and Peredur's puddings is unbelievable!

'WOW!' says the mayor, 'I don't care about puddings or desserts any more, I only want to eat these new Puddserts!'

'YEAH! Who cares about puddings or desserts. Puddserts are way better!' says Mel the Member of Parliament.

OPEN
OPEN

Delwen and Peredur look at each other and realise they have created something even better than puddings or desserts... the Puddsert!

'Well... perhaps you aren't so bad after all. Sorry for being a pernicious pudding person,' says Delwen.

'Well, perhaps your desserts are pretty top notch. Sorry for being a dessert dictator,' says Peredur.

They knock down the wall between the two shops and create a new temple of treats – That Puddsert Place – which sells the best puddserts in the entire milky way!

The whole town flocks to the shop to eat the banana split milkshakes, the apple pie sundaes and the lemon drizzle forest gateaus.

'Dessert + Pudding = Puddsert,' says Ceri.

'Puddsert + Belly = TASTY!' says Deri.

'Delwen + Peredur = AWESOME!' says everyone!

PUDDSERT
PLACE
OPEN

Ceri & Deri

Ceri & Deri
NO TIME FOR CLOCKS
Max Low
GRAFFEG

Ceri & Deri
THE TREASURE MAP
Max Low
GRAFFEG

Ceri & Deri
BUILD A BIRDHOUSE
Max Low
GRAFFEG

Ceri & Deri
GOOD TO BE SWEET
Max Low
GRAFFEG

Ceri & Deri
YOUNG WHIPPERSNAPPER
MAX LOW

Ceri & Deri
THE VERY SMELLY TELLY SHOW!
MAX LOW
on

Ceri & Deri
GET YOUR SKATES ON
MAX LOW
GRAFFEG

Ceri & Deri
PUDDING FOR DESSERT
MAX LOW
GRAFFEG